Bella dancerella™

Bella and the Beast

8

Written by

Poppy Rose

ABC
Books

Illustrated by

Omar Aranda

Bella and the animals were crowded into the farmhouse attic. 'Do you *really* want to hear about the adventure Roy and I had in the magical land of Tututopia, *again*?'

'We love hearing about how you and Roy went through the mirror into another world,' Agatha clucked.

'Well,' Bella began, 'I turned the key in the lock of Mum's jewellery box and two drawers popped open.'

'And there was a bracelet in one drawer,' quacked Puddles.

'And the shape of a tiny wand cut into a piece of foam in the second drawer,' honked Waddles.

3

'Bella!' Dad called from the landing. 'Charlotte's mother was just on the phone. She wants you to partner with Charlotte for the duet exam at the State Ballet Company.'

'*No way!*' Bella cried. 'I'm dancing with Annalise. Why would Charlotte want to partner with me, anyway?

She's been such a beastie to me. I don't think she likes me very much at all.'

'Well, her mum wants her to partner with you,' Dad replied, giving Bella a wink. 'I told her you'd talk to Charlotte about it at ballet class tomorrow.'

'Why would I partner with Charlotte?' Bella said, flopping onto the attic floor again. 'First, she took Mum's tiara from my bag and broke it. Then she took my lucky ribbon because she knew it was lucky.'

'Charlotte's mum probably thinks Charlotte will get a better mark if she dances the duet with you,' woofed Roy.

'I don't know about that, but I do know I won't be dancing with beastly Charlotte,' Bella said firmly.

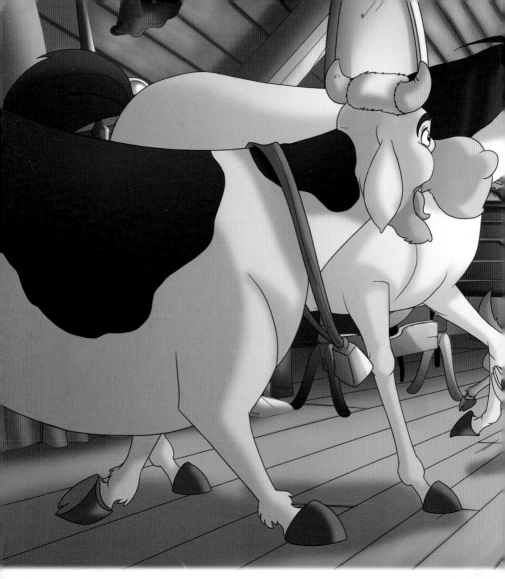

'Back to the story now,' squeaked Maggie. 'You were up to the moment you put the bracelet on.'

'And I closed the clasp,' Bella continued. 'At the same time, the mirror started to *shimmer* and Roy and I went through it into a magical land.'

'How did Roy get to go with you?' bleated Chloe. 'He wasn't wearing a bracelet.'

'I think Roy went with me because he had his paw on my leg as I closed the clasp,' Bella answered. 'We were connected.'

All at once the animals rushed to be as close to Bella as they could get.

'Everybody off!' Bella chuckled.

'**Look**!' woofed Roy. 'Another drawer has just opened.'

'What's in there?' mooed Mimmee.

'A tiara charm,' Bella answered, peering into the drawer. 'And I think it has the letter $\mathscr{B}$ on it.'

'Time to go!' called a little white mouse, who Bella hadn't seen since her adventure in Tututopia. He scurried across the floor into Bella's lap.

'What are you doing here, my little Tututopian friend?'
Bella asked as she picked up the tiara charm.

Instantly, the mirror began to *shimmer* and Bella, the
family of mice and the Tututopian mouse went through it.

Bella and the mice landed in a pile of soft, mushy leaves.
'We're in a forest,' Bella whispered, looking about.

'It's so gloomy and scary here,' squeaked Maggie. 'And
who is *this* mouse? He doesn't live on our farm.'

'I'm Sebastian and I live in Tututopia,' the little white mouse
said. 'I'm to stay with Bella for as long as she needs me.'

'Is this spooky forest part of Tututopia, Sebastian?'
Bella asked.

Sebastian scratched his head. 'We're in the Kingdom
of Enchantment, but I've never seen it like this. It's
always so pretty and sunny. It's one of my favourite
kingdoms. But not today!'

'Hey! The tiara charm has changed into a real tiara,' Bella gasped. 'But what's that whispering noise I can hear?'

'It's the trees and the plants whispering about us,' Sebastian answered as the family of mice climbed into Bella's pocket. 'This is an enchanted forest, remember.'

'Are the things in the enchanted forest friendly?' Bella asked in a whisper, placing the tiara on her head.

A terrible screeching began. '*That* doesn't sound friendly,' Sebastian squeaked. 'And it's getting louder!'

'It's wolves!' Bella gulped, breaking into a run.

'They're gaining on us!' Maggie squeaked, peering out from Bella's pocket.

Without warning, tree branches began swooping down around Bella. 'What are they doing?' Bella screamed, trying to leap over them.

'I think they want to help, Bella,' Sebastian said.
'They're trying to pick you up.'

As Bella slowed down, the tree branches swept
her up. Higher and higher they took her, away
from the growling wolves.

As Bella reached the highest branch, the whole tree shook from an almighty ROAAARR below. Bella turned to see a massive beast scaring the wolves away. And as she did, her foot slipped and she fell. The tiara slid from her head.

'AAARGH!' Bella spluttered, clutching the mice to her as she fell down into the massive beast's arms, the tiara following, landing crookedly on her head.

As Bella gawped open-mouthed at the creature holding her, the beast stared intently at the tiara. 'You are safe with me,' the beast assured Bella with a surprisingly gentle growl. 'We will go to my castle.'

Inside the castle, the beast carefully placed Bella on a seat near the fire.

'It's Beauty's beast,' Sebastian said, leaping into the beast's palm. 'Have we been brought here because of what's happened to the forest?'

The beast let out a sigh, shoulders sagging, eyes fixed on the flames of the fire.

'You look so sad,' Bella said. 'It's more than just the dark and gloomy forest, isn't it? Tell us everything.'

'Someone has cast an evil spell over our magical forest,'
the beast began. 'The wolves that live here are usually
friendly, but the spell has changed them and made
them mean.'

'Who would have done this?' Bella asked.

'I don't know,' the beast answered. 'But worse than this,
my lovely Beauty has disappeared. She left here to visit

her father on the other side of the forest and she hasn't returned. We have a performance at the Royal Opera House in London very soon. I can't change from a beast into her prince without her.'

'Perhaps she stayed with her father because the forest was too *scary* to walk through,' Bella suggested.

The beast took Bella and the mice to a mirror that hung on the castle wall. 'This mirror allows me to see Beauty and keep her safe,' the beast said, lifting Bella up. 'There's Beauty leaving her father's place to come home, but she hasn't made it back to the castle.'

'Look and see where she is now,' Bella suggested.

'I can't,' the beast sighed. 'The mirror can't show me anything any more because the evil spell is blocking it. It's stopping the trees, plants and me from helping Beauty. But maybe you can help her.'

'You had to rescue *me* from the wolves!' Bella exclaimed. 'How can I help Beauty in that forest?'

'Bella means beautiful,' the beast explained. 'Bella, Beauty and a tiara with a $\mathcal{B}$ on it that fits you perfectly. You must be here to bring her home.'

'But we can't go back out into that scary forest again!' squeaked Maggie.

Bella bit her bottom lip and looked into the mirror once more. And as she did, the dark clouds that filled it began to clear. 'I can see myself in the mirror now.'

'And the tiara is starting to glow!' cried Sebastian.

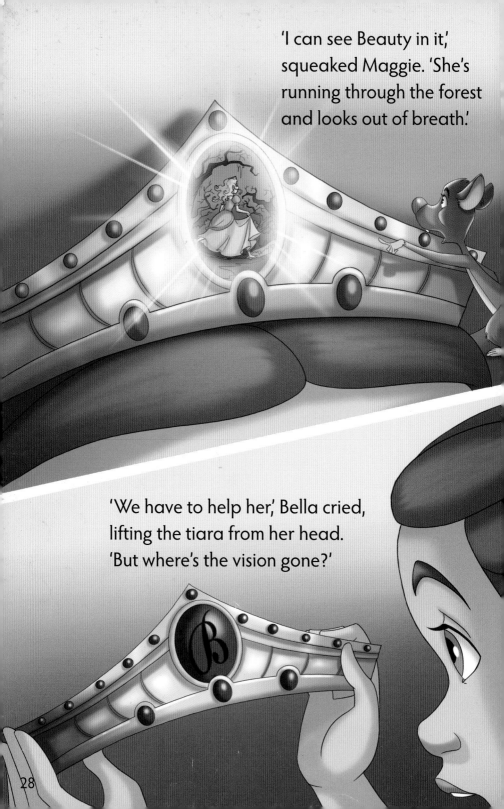

'I can see Beauty in it,' squeaked Maggie. 'She's running through the forest and looks out of breath.'

'We have to help her,' Bella cried, lifting the tiara from her head. 'But where's the vision gone?'

'I know how magic works,' said the beast, walking Bella
to the castle door. 'The tiara will show you Beauty
only when you're wearing it, Bella. The glow is already
starting to fade. When it has faded completely, time
has run out. You must leave now. **Hurry!**'

The tiara showed Beauty surrounded by ferns.

Bella got lost in the tunnels
and took some wrong turns.

Beauty ran from the ferns and into wild flowers.

Bella searched in that garden for hours and hours.

The fading tiara showed Beauty climbing a tall tree.

But the wolves had found Bella and she had to flee.

When the tiara stopped glowing,
the visions stopped too.

They hadn't found Beauty
and returned feeling blue.

The group trudged miserably through the castle doors. 'I'm so, so sorry,' Bella sobbed.

'You did your best, but my Beauty is lost and the ballet is doomed,' groaned the beast.

As Bella looked up at the beast, the tiara began to glow once more.

'The tiara's unleashing new magic,' Sebastian said.
'Play some music from the *Beauty and the Beast* ballet!'

As the family of mice played, magic whooshed from
the tiara and winded its way over Bella.

'You've been transformed into Beauty!' the beast
stammered as he danced with Bella.

And all at once, they were gone.

On centre stage at the London Royal Opera House, Bella danced with the beast. Trapped in their own spell, they were enchanting.

'Thank you for saving the ballet,' the beast whispered as they danced.

'You're more than welcome,' Bella replied happily.

'I just wish that I could have saved Beauty as well.'

'When we return to Tututopia, we'll think of a way to save her,' the beast assured Bella. 'But for now, we must perform.'

'This tiara truly is magical,' Bella whispered. 'I know every step without thinking! Perhaps it holds more magic still.'

Then the tiara shone and showered the beast in a dusting of *magic*. The audience cheered as the beast was transformed into a handsome prince.

Bella gasped at the change that took place before her. *There's nothing beastly about him at all*, she thought.

As Bella and the prince took their bows, a vision of
Charlotte and her mother popped into Bella's head,
but she had no time to wonder why. The curtains
quickly closed, and Bella and the prince were gone.

Back at the castle, Bella gasped. 'You've gone back to being a beast,' she said to the beast as someone burst through the castle door. 'And Beauty's made it home at last!'

Everyone rushed to Beauty, relieved to see her safe and sound.

'When Bella danced with you, she unleashed pure magic from the tiara,' Beauty explained. 'It transformed you and broke the spell over the Kingdom of Enchantment. The wolves are friendly once more and the forest is sunny and magical.'

Bella and the mice moved to the windows. 'It's gorgeous!' Bella cried. 'It really is a beautiful kingdom you live in.'

Bella turned to Beauty, puzzled. 'You remind me of someone, Beauty,' she mused. 'I just can't quite think who.'

In a flash, Bella realised it was Charlotte and she suddenly understood why she'd been so beastly.

It was all the pressure from her mum. *Perhaps Charlotte isn't all she seems either*, Bella thought.

As these thoughts ran through Bella's mind, the tiara shrank and attached itself to her bracelet, then Bella and the mice were gone.

Back in the attic, the animals were where they had been when Bella and the mice left. 'We saw you go through the mirror and come back, but no time has passed in between,' neighed Jasper.

'You've had another adventure in Tututopia and this time the mice went with you!' woofed Roy.

'**Yes!**' cried Bella. 'And it was incredible, but the
mice can tell you all about it. There is someone
I must call straight away.'

'And there's someone you all must meet,' squeaked
Maggie, chest puffed out. 'Our family of mice has
a new member. Farm animals, meet Sebastian. He
has come to stay with us for a while from Tututopia.'

45

Outside the testing rooms of the State Ballet Company, Bella was busy cutting her lucky ribbon into three equal pieces. 'A lucky ribbon for all three of us!' She beamed. 'Thanks for giving it back to me, Charlotte.'

'Thank you so much for this and for talking to Miss Honeywell for me,' Charlotte said. 'All three of us dancing

the exam together, and with lucky ribbons in our hair!
I feel so guilty about the way I've behaved. I've been
positively beastly, Bella, and I'm really sorry.'

Bella toyed with the tiara charm on her bracelet and
smiled. 'I'm sorry too, Charlotte,' she replied. 'When
Mum died, Dad said I was beastly for ages afterwards.'

'We all have bad moments, Charlotte, but it doesn't mean we're awful or mean,' Bella said firmly. 'We're going to be the *best* of friends from now on. We'll look out for each other and help each other. And we'll dance this exam brilliantly!'